OUT OF THE FLAMES

OUT OF THE FLAMES

POEMS BY LYN DALEBOUT

Blue Bison
P r e s s

For

Wanda and Mel Dalebout

and

Yellowstone and Grand Teton National Parks

Library of Congress Catalog Card Number 96-95234

ISBN 0-9655247-0-1

TABLE OF CONTENTS

OUT OF THE FLAMES

STARS

YELLOWSTONE

JOY

Out of the Flames

OUT OF THE FLAMES

For Yellowstone Park and the fires of 1988

STARS:
Ancient fire
coming down from the sky
imprinting the future
upon the folds of the Earth.

YELLOWSTONE:
Currents of fire
pushing up from the ground
—a reborn planet—
imprinting the present
upon the People.

JOY:
Just this
—an airborne intuition,
maybe the wind singing—
You
are in charge of changing
the whole
world.

STARS

THE WIND IS THE SPIN

This wind
is the planet swirling
faster and faster

yet no one notices,
too busy are we
with the life of our choice

which is not of our choosing,
so bound are we
to the rules, by the rules.

Until we honor the wind,
we will never know the secret
rules of this Earth.

We will be bound, will be
bound
by our past

caught in the trap
of family.

For family is meant to be
an open door,
like the wind, forgiving,
always new, always new.
An open door we walk through,
always new, always new.

The wind,
it's picking up now.
Tonight I fear it will
rid my house of its roof

and I will be open to the sky—
rid of protection
at last!
Safe beneath the stars.

But my fear is:
I will be free

of my shell, my home,
of the family I've known

and I'll have to face the stars,
their vulnerability:

our great connectedness.

I listen to this wind
for in the end
it is what will last,
it will outlast even gravity.

For the wind
it is the spin
of our Earth,
our true home,
the family
for which we long.

ANTELOPE DREAMING

I run across these open plains
    as if I were an antelope
and needed no trail, only the wind.

I strike out across snow and these open places
    to return home at night. In spring
I never sink in and run like a coyote,
    homeward, with the wind.

It is my good fortune, and through many prayers,
    that I can walk all the way to Yellowstone,
if I had to, across open flats, like a river of wind.

I rise above the ground, like the marsh hawks,
    returning in spring, diving with their young,
as if the air had hollows, loopholes, hidden
    entrances and exits only they could see.

It is my good fortune to live in Wyoming,
    a state so empty of human diversion
that we are a black hole at night on the satellite maps.

We are broadcasting space, and we are broadcasting
    open space, and there is a silence to be heard
in Wyoming, and that's what we are here to do.

A place to counteract the noise and artificial light
    of those who have forgotten the night,
the place of dreaming. The antelope are dreaming now,
    I am sure, as I walk home across the space of

Dark Wyoming reflecting back the sky of nighttime.
    What if there were no stars, like in those mapped
cities of night? It would be like seeing with no sight,
    it would be unholy, maybe natural to another planet

But not this one of antelope dreaming
    Wyoming into existence, breathing the notion of a state
large and empty and silent and observant.

Sit down before the last stars go out
    a billion years from now.
Sense how already, it has already ended.

The Yeis, the Listeners

Tonight, near midnight
I walked under a full moon,
all things equal inside
made even by tears.

This night, I was taught by moonlight
to be the Yei
and bend toward the Moon's
white rhythmic waves.

My body bent like half a rainbow,
curved toward the moon,
curved like a woman.
I am a woman, and I like to listen.

"No more talk! Too much noise!
Too many words circulating the planet.

Time to listen.
Time to listen.

It's in the wind, the sound of gravity
the earth shifting beneath your feet."

The Yeis, they bend as flowers bend,
toward the light and they are listening,
that's why they bend, that's why there's Life,
in bending and in listening.

THE OLDEST THING WE KNOW

The oldest thing we know is Mystery.
The oldest thing Spirit was is Mystery.
Now we have Beauty
as Mystery settles into Form.
But the oldest thing we know is Mystery.

DREAMING OF SAPPHIRE CORN

The corn was a string of Christmas lights,
    royal blue and shimmering.
The corn was a string of sapphires
    with red fire talking inside.

So out of place in the grocery case
    of governed vegetables
already told what to do by their genes.

THIS CORN

was beyond the DNA,
    or housed a new secret
at the center of its cells,
    alerting me to iridescence.

This corn sang
    and carried the night sky
packed in every kernel.
    It spoke without words

of why the holy lives
    in all living forms
and moves more quietly in the
    inorganic worlds, sparkling.

To dream of vegetables
    is in no book I know,
but the blue corn ears
    speak to me

as I await their return
    to this reality.

Virus

The viruses will take you out
if you're not careful.

If Life
keeps seeing you obsessing on
your self,
your beliefs,
your behalf,
your own sector of the tribal truth,

well, viruses have come
as crystalline, reverent orbs
to remind us

that we are the same:
biological organisms, as they are
    biological jewels,
that's the way
we are one.

Better listen to the viruses

who are states of energy
more than organism,
who are border creatures
sent to take us out

if we won't listen

to the one Lifeforce
growing us all toward
our individual perfection.

THE HALF LIFE

Have you heard
children laugh four hundred times a day
and adults
maybe fifteen? That constitutes

the half life,
the quarter life,
or no life at all.

Life is
taking me back
to the first origins.
More consciously this time.
I appear normal, but really

I'm a traveling, enlightened coin
rolling around the universe,
traversing planetary orbits,
tracing eye-orbed saints,
trying to learn the new beginnings,
trying to remember
the origins
of love.

BLUE PLANET

For Lee Klinger

I have a blue heart.
It is the size of the
Blue Whale, or this Blue Planet
to which it listens.
It sits right here
on the right side of my chest.

With the blue heart
I listen to the other worlds.
It's how I learn of those
different from myself.

There's no such thing as normal.
That's what the blue heart knows,
for it has lived before
and beat in other bodies, other species,
rocks alive!

The blue heart informs the red heart,
which is the heart of action.
Can you feel them in your chest,
the blue heart listening,
the red heart acting?

Can you feel these worlds
wrapped around each other,
intertwined as lovers?

Can you feel them in your chest
these hearts of listening,
hearts of passion acting
on Blue's behalf?

I have a blue heart which sits
right here
and is the size of the Blue planet
to which it listens.

THE GREAT LISTENING

The animals know
when to come to us
because they are
knowingly linked
by the web of listening.
Without thinking
they are always listening.

The miracle motions
of birds flocking
turning left, turning right,
they've not forgotten
how to listen
to the Great Listening.

The Great Listening
goes on beneath our feet,
above our heads,
inside our hearts.
And the animals swirl
in delightful fashion.

They seem to move
before the wind moves them,
as if they knew the future
and were bringing it back to us.

They let themselves be moved.
They hear the Great Thoughts
circling this Earth,
the larger language
circling this Earth.

They transmit messages
because they're listening
without thinking
and we can learn from them
by watching movements
scribbled in the Earth,
above our heads,
inside our hearts.

The animals know
when to come to us
when we are listening
without thinking.
Like them
we are linked by listening
without thinking
linked by listening.

BEAR PAW

I scheduled five days
in the depth of winter
in the heart of Yellowstone

hoping to bring back gifts:
the overheard dreams of
bears.

These thrumming voices
were the disturbed paws of
Bear
beating the ground
drumming the sound
older than war
into our hearts.

There is something
older than war,
and we must remember.

Obsidian I

It is the universal statement of a star,
the message Orion
has carried
in winter
through the ages:

It is the dark
which illuminates.

EARTH STONE

If you feel into the sky,
   bowl of stars,
you will travel far beyond duality.

If you are willing

to feel into the stars,
   bowl of sky,
you can feel safe again

not trapped on Earth,
or split by distance
to the Sun.

Whole,
as stone of peach
resides inside:
hard
home
seed.

Seed is center
to the flesh,
and seed is dead
without the juice
of Life

as

peach is dead
without hard seed,

both are central
and in the center

as is this bowl of sky
to human brain:
trapped or central.

Juice and seed,
both are central,
both are life
in different forms.

One is now,
one is future
both are life
both in the center.

If you feel into the sky,
to realm of Being,
like animals,
the stars cry out their leanings
in a tongue rejoined.

The Milky Way
is Mystery's tongue,
if we had the ears to hear.

If we had the ears to hear.

YELLOWSTONE

CALDERA

For Lake Yellowstone

Caldera comes singing.
    Lights out!
    A blown fuse!
    Vast night   six hundred thousand years ago.

Caldera comes singing.
    New life
    can come into
    the region!

Caldera comes singing!
    Announcing TODAY
    in her explosive
    virgin tongue.

        "I will scatter the bones
        of this region so far
            that stories will have to be told.

        I will make
        the people speak."

Caldera comes singing.
    Recalling the scattered blood
    of six hundred thousand years
    ago.

Obsidian II

It was Summer Solstice
and I felt the cancer forming in my breast.
Too many stories of stagnation.
I got instructions in June
to quit in December
at the Winter Solstice

and to take time off
and listen to my small plot of greens
and perennials
and not to read anymore
all the books of pain

and to be with friends
and tend to family
but not in the sick way
but in the way of slowing down
to the point of
being
together.

And so I listened for the words
that are more the shape of something,
like weather is a language,
a slow sure tongue
always dropping the future
at our feet.

IN THE BEAR VOICE

Have you heard
the rushing leaves of water,
a bullion over aspen,
reflections and the mirrored firs,
all falling silently together
toward the ocean
collapsing in
one upon the other
in a deafening rush of color?

This is what I see as Bear.
This is my definition of gravity.
Riparian and raucous,
the ritual of Fall.

Come away from the edge of your wall
of belief,
a fence of fire burning needlessly.
Try
for our sake
to step away from your ancient fear
and hear what we have to say.

We've Always shared the Earth.
We've always Shared the Earth.

Here first, long before you.
Saw sights
you'll never see.
Ask us of history.
Ask us what we know
of biology.

Name

You know what
mystery
is beauty
and beauty
to be so close
to the truth,

your truth
which you live so closely.

You don't even know
its rules,
your game.

I am awed
in your presence.
Wind-filled hawk,
the cobbled fish,
on course,
knowing no other.

Given choice
we learn
there is none
to our name.

Coyote is border,
antelope, wind.

And so we must
learn again
who we are.

EMBRACING BEAR

When I told the man
of my desire
to embrace the bear,
his words of
violent caution
told all:

Get over it!

He pulls out a picture
of a huge grizzly bear
gnawing on a red carcass.
He scoffs at my dream
to hold a bear.

Driven underground
this same desire
spawns poetry
or war.

So, I tell the
man of my desire
to embrace the Bear!

Inside, the Bear ravages for new fruit!
Inside, the Bear continues to shred the
            inside of his heart.
Inside, the Bear scrapes my womb each month
            and so I bleed.

Inside, the Bear's alive!

And we are locked
in love or combat,
raw embrace.

Most Faces are Asymmetric

That my heart
doesn't follow the determined
course of anatomy
pounds arrhythmically   unpredictably

he discovered one night   awake
my sleeping head to his chest
his open hand to my heart.

At our unhappy ending
I was abandoned to my
heart's eurhythmic voice
I had no choice

and he was left
to his insomnia:
erratic   unused breath.

CLOISTERED

It is dusk.
Grey has descended
black's not far off
the ground white
only because of snow.

Cobalt nets the air.

It is dusk.
White steam rising
through a rainbow of greys.
I am standing before
Old Faithful,
beginning to sing
softly.

Stop   suddenly

as sixteen miniature monks
head toward me,
or so I think.

I can't imagine what they are.

Grey has ended now
almost black
cobalt all around.

I can imagine what they are.

They move solemnly forward
short steps
completely timed
to one another.
Correct pause.
When one stops short
they all stop short
with meandering coos.

We all breathe in the silence
breathe in silence
pause together
for an instant
we are in union
the sixteen hooded monks
or so I imagine them to be.

So softly their walking prayers
ground this earth.
So soundlessly their steps
shelter true sanity.
So silently
they go their way.....true saints.

Then   one flies up sharply   with squawk!

I know that sound
to be geese
and my eyes break open now.

I see the black hoods
and white necks of daylight.
My eyes caught in reality
cannot turn back
to see the hidden imagery
I can no longer imagine.

Mystery's been shattered.
I stand longing to know
the unknown again.

I am never sure which world
I'd prefer to inhabit.

JOURNEY

If you stare out a window
you came to be quiet by,
what's on the other side
is not necessarily what you see.

My eyes drift passed
the barrack buildings of Yellowstone,
passed elk grazing
scared to cross the paved straight road
while cars rush too quickly by.

My eyes reach farther than the
northeast edge of Yellowstone,
dart through the vast expanse of mid-Wyoming
into the red heart
of the Black Hills
and there, come to rest.

I have journeyed thus.
You probably have too.

We do so much
we were not trained
to understand.
There is so much
we were trained not
to understand.

HOLY WATER

There are wretched holes in Yellowstone
resembling old wounds in need of healing.
Places to watch the unguarded imagination.

Sulphur coffins, grottos where we hide
our oldest secrets, the unremembered memories
dripping   silently   endlessly   inside.

Graves of ancestors, habits hard lived in me,
dying to die. With me, all the old is reborn,
all the good and the difficult.

A varicose listening. Pieces of the past,
like unbedded ghosts, trying to live,
because they have not yet been put to rest.

And, in Yellowstone there are fragrant
blue-bound waters from deep within the Earth.
An explosion of blue listening!

Depression Geyser has deepened
and fallen into itself.

Beehive Geyser streaked with cornflower blue
warns "Stand by for growth!"

Ear Spring.
"Listen. Speaking loudly is not our way."
Blue Owl Geyser
sapphired eyes of night, inner sight.

Oracle Pool
sings of the ever present give away.

Blue Star Spring
full of old bison bones softening dissolving.

CEREMONY

For Boiling River

This dryland bone of death
I brought to break
was eaten clean.
The hawk hovered last spring.

I'll probably throw
it toward the Gardner River--
River of Cobalt Beam--
which will give it to the Yellowstone, I hope
for that is where I'd like these wishes to go.

But maybe,
it will settle downstream
from the Boiling River--
the River That Breaks Bones--
and be cloaked in emerald satin
of teaming algae, and soon
resemble itself no longer.

Soon a fish will nibble away
the bone's coat of green
and once again,
it will be eaten clean,
this time by water.

Then kicked loose by crossing elk,
this time, floats toward the Yellowstone--
River of Viridescent Rose--
washed clean and free

for that is how
I'd like to be.

PRESENCE OF MIND

Nature,
at last,
brings me no peace.
Everywhere I look
I see the rugged struggle:
ducks buffeted by wind,
elk running from me!
a prayerful person!

I see too much in things.
Read too much into life.
At the river
I find nothing I want to know
only the ceaseless, restless
cycling of things.

I come here today
and see nothing I could call
beauty.
Only wholeness, everywhere I look
wholeness.

GHOST HORSE

Wind whistling through windowed cracks,
   with the fury of a silenced elder,
     with the force of children running from war,

is like a horde of ancient ghosts
     coming to hound you
       into a dream not of your making

with a language unstructured and true
     as the music. Wind voicing itself
       through cracks, walls,

can drive you mad
     because it's saying something, by god,
       it's trying to tell you Something

but it feels more like an order,
     chastisement, and it wails for
       something you never did,

but it pulls at you,
     tugs at your consciousness of
     the unconsciousness

we all have,
     because there are so many promises
     we have broken.

CROSS FIRE

The elk pool at dusk
await the word of light
going down
await the dark.

They travel like
slow moving lightening
across Antelope Flats
awaiting dark coming down.
We see their instincts strong
as they've learned
to move at night.

We wait with them
and keep a silent vigil
for safe passage.
While we offer refuge,
first they must cross
fire, the shooting gallery
which lines their way
to safety.

We hope they are protected
from this hunt
which is not a hunt.
It's a betrayal
of an ancient pact
which is the hunt.
This is not a hunt.
It is betrayal.

The Whole of our Surroundings

When I met with Sitting Bull
sitting on Shadow Mountain
gazing west and listening
to the whole of his surroundings,
there was a peace about him
about what he'd done,
was about to do,
what he'd live through,
which I already knew
coming from his future.

Yet he informed me,
spoke to me
of what was ahead.
And he said to make our peace
with the coming times.

So long ago, so long ahead
he sees with the whole of his surroundings,
the soundings of his surroundings.
He is alone. He is alive.
He is surrounded.

So he surrendered to his day,
to his history, the myth
that must unfold.
He moved back and forth
between past and now,
past and future.

He came to be at peace
before returning to his people.

One story became
his Myth of Path—
the myth of past, his story.
The other gift,
his Mythic Vision—
a myth of future.

Reaching toward me   now
both inform me   past and future
of what's coming   now.
He was praying for our future
because this was to be his last story
the way of history.

What I will remember from our speaking
with the whole of our surroundings
is that we were listening
all at once
to past   present   future.

And all we knew
was we must
find our Source
of peace
for the coming time.

O Bison

Speak to me.
I want to know
if there was any joy
near the end

or were you forced to forget
even the weather
that was always
a soft blanket
to your skins,
frigid, or under the
frothing heat of summer,
a protection.

O Bison....
I think of your herds,
your tens of thousands,
and how you spoke
in a hundred ways
to one another
and took the things you needed
only
when it was necessary.

O Bison....
I wonder if we people
ever feel how light
and tender are our skins

next to your toughness
and sinewed network
of fur like earth,
your vanished light.

THIS BIAS AGAINST BISON

1. My feet went walking
in another world
to discover the roots
of this bias against the Bison.

I was barefoot
walking in green grass
in high grass
under a blue sky
an infinitely high
blue sky.

I felt the spirit of the Bison
everywhere.
I was walking amongst
the ghost herds,
sixty million ghosts
of rumbling Bison.

I heard their spirit laughter:
breath of bounty
breath of trusting spirit
breath in knowing all their needs were met.

These were the chosen Bison
trusting the People
giving to the People
in their time of need
still thundering
still breathing quietly amongst their kin

the whole herd
one big kin.

These Bison are returning here
as they once returned
to the spirit world
where I hear them now
rustling, walking,
breathing.

It takes us here to call them back,
to welcome them home
as history, in continual reversal,
asserts itself again.

They are ready. They've wandered
long enough beneath perfect skies.
They want the Earth again.
They want the Earth beneath their feet again.
They seek our help.
They need our help to return them
to the Earth again.

For they are there.
I heard them in the other world.
I await their words.

2. They say they will forgive us
for their slaughter.
Sixty million dead in simply months.
They say some had to leave
for times were dark

as history spiraled to its death.
There would be no place for them,
the place they held:
of bounty and of prayer.
They would have smothered
no b r e a t h   no b r e a t h
no room to breathe.

They say there are still no words,
but that we've grown used to
senseless slaughter--
the downside of our species.

Unrelenting domination.
Unbearable disconnection.
We think the way to peace
is bloody war.

3. "You're cracking open.
There is a joy returning.
There will be too much light
for some to stay.

We want the Earth again.
We want the Earth beneath our feet again.
If you do not love this Earth
and all her bounty,
then please, remove yourselves,
do not stay.

If you do not love this place
with all your heart

then give it back to us

who fertilized Her unfailingly--
perhaps our greatest gift!--
and grunted the daily language of
thank you!
and of prayer.

Our solo grunts and rumblings,
our massive tribal thunderings,
it was all applause,
all applause
for the universal bounty,
the unEarthly beauty
of this place.

You never knew, but now you know.
You always guessed, but now you know.
It was all applause,
our glad communion with the Earth."

4. My feet went walking
in another world
to discover the roots of bias
against Bison.

They say they will forgive us.
They would provide again
these thundering nations.

For they are there.
We need them here.
They await our word.

BONES

They honor the past:
Deeds.
They are dead,
once full of life,
now full of spirit.
Ribcage chalice to the Sky.
Cloud spines draping over the Earth.

They are porous to
anOther world.
They draw us into theirs:
our hands reach through
and listen to bone stories
--sad but true--
where history has already
taught forgiveness.

Who knows who we've been.
Or what we've done.
Or which side we've been on.

It's from these bones
and all their history
  --the matrixed space,
    their ivory quiet--
that we will learn.

JOY

THE BEAR SONG

Bear down
Bear down
Bear down
Bear goes down
Bear goes down
Bear goes down to give birth
Bear goes down to fall asleep
Bear down into the depths to hibernate
Bear hibernates through the dark time
Bear goes deep down
Bear goes deep down
Bear goes deep
Bear goes deep
Bear   goes   deep

Bear goes to sleep
Bear goes to sleep
      goes to sleep
Bear breathes
     barely breathing
Bear breathes
     barely breathing
Bear breathes

breathes   breathes   breathes
breath   breath   breath
bre   bre   bre   bre
br br br
brrrrrrrrrrrrr   brrrrrrrrrrrrrr   brrrrrrrrrrrrrrrrrrrrrrrrrrrr

Bear breathes us through
breathes us through
Bear breathes us through
the ice age of every winter
the death of every winter
the deaths of each winter
the solitude of winter
the loneliness of winter
the emptiness   emptiness

Bear breathes in us rebirth
Bear breathes us to rebirth
Bear breathes us through the birth
Bear breathes us through the birth

Bear down
       Bear down
          Bear down

Bear dreams us up
      dreams us up
Bear dreams us up

Dream   Dream   Dream
dr   dr   dr   dr
drrrrrrrrrrrrrrrrrrrrrrrrrrrrrrrrrrrrrrr
Drum Drum Drum
Drum Drum Drum
Drum Drum Drum

Bear drums in us
Bear drums in us the spring

Bear drums us into spring

Bear paws drum us into spring
Bears' paw drums us into spring

Bear paws down under drum
Bears' paw down under drums
Bear paws down under drum
Bears' paw down under drums

And dreams and drums and breathes
and dreams and drums and breathes and
dreams and drums and breathes and dreams and drums

breathes dreams drums breathes dreams drums breathes
dreams drums breathes dreams drums breathes dreams
drumsbreathesdreamsdrumsbreathesdreamsdrumsbreaths

till birth is given
till birth is given
till birth is given
dreamsdrumsbreathesdreamsdrumsbreathesdreamsdrums-
breathes

till breath is given
till breath is given
till
breath
is
given

Obsidian III

It came to me
this summer
on Obsidian Mountain
through glint of black shadowed chips
shining in the sun
and buried underground,
it came to me, our mission:
free-ranging citizens,
boiling ourselves in hot springs,
risking contamination,
moving between galaxies and Gaia,
stars and buried diamonds,
mercurial,
awaiting messages.

THE WORK OF THE NIGHT

Awakened at 2 a.m
to the sound of wings
within my darkened stovepipe.
Something is frantic
to get out,
tubed in black, caught in creosote
under a full moon,
white.

Helpless at 2:30
there's nothing I can do
not knowing if what I hear
is bird or rodent
scratching for release,
neither of us knowing
the way out.

Morning
I look within
and shine a flashlight
and a prayer
to guide it down.

Three hours later
a blackened bluebird
flutters down.
Through cast iron door the bird
flies out and jettisons
to the window.

I guide it out
to a gentle rain waiting
to wash its wings.

My stovepipe
now cleansed
stands safe for new fires.

PORTRAIT AT DAWN

He is a high glaciered brow
but low down, the rivered saint.

Instinctive eyes, he
sees beneath the surface of things,
eggs inside the river's edge.

He stopped apologizing
years ago yet
withholds his interior self
like a river stone.
Life flows over his waiting.
He listens.
He is a good listener.

Looking sidewise
he glances back
to notice ripples, dimples
of a childhood left behind.

He'll crop up someday.
He'll turn from stone
to Raven,
one night when no one's looking,
while he's asleep.
He'll be surprised one morning
when he awakens
with wings.

Treetop, wingtip,
far-reaching.
Broad, high expanse
of thought beyond thought.

So white will be his eyesight.
So clear blue, his heart.

Contemporary Aboriginal

Breathing, water, walking, hands and silence.

Ancient tools
to make us whole.
Seeds to sow
a present soul.

Constant change,
constant change.
Read both ways.
Replenishment.

The tribes of Yellowstone
carry only these.
Their packs are empty,
full of these.

Breathing, water, walking, hands and silence.

BIRDSONG

Writing that sings like a song.
Different than poetry,
language of gods.
Writing that sings like a song.
Melodic and rhythmic, alive with sound,
and constantly touching the heart.

Instrumentation:
Woodwinds and logs.
Pounding of creeks,
bounding of dogs.
Musical notes
written on air.
Birds are the wavelengths,
lightening stairs.

Birds hear the truth.
Convey it at dawn.
Changing the climate.
Threshold of song.

LONGING AND LATITUDE

1. Sleeping out in August, stepping under
the blueblack blanket bearing down,
the night sky Perseid shower bears down.
Stars, laying like the wind,
lightly covering me
the Moon blanket
so I can sleep   wide awake.
Eyes open and closed
at the same time. That's
dreams, they are the same
as night vision.
Eyes open and closed
all at once!
Seeing the same thing
in both worlds.
Night is the time
of no separation.

2. The Milky Way
started out
north to south   south to north
at dusk, star-streaked.

By dawn
was spiraling
east to west   west to east

granting
longitude and latitude.

3. You   east of me now
were north a month ago. I sent you
messages at dusk   south to north
casting the fibered sky
with waves of Longitude.
Dreaming you, I imagine you
and ask you   please
to visit.

4. Now   you are east of me
and Latitude befriends us,
carries words we want to say.

I hear you whisper
"good morning." I hear the words
east to west
as tongue of sky   the Milky Way
aligns my dreams.

5. I hear the words
more true
with Latitude

unlike the Longitude
which tracks the silence
in the heart.

6. The Milky Way
I always knew
was prototype
to satellite...
solitude.

But it is you,
standing there
dreaming me upon the Earth
that lets me trust the use of galaxies
to track our dreams.

THIRTEEN MOONS

Thirteen moons. Only
twelve months.
Something's been lost,
something's been lost.

Thirteen perfect moons.
Twelve uneven months.
Something's been changed,
something's been changed.

Tampered time.
We've forgotten its radial nature
shooting out in all directions.
Like light,
time does not confine
but shines through us all.

Time is money   or
time is art.

Time serves art,
money should serve time,

Art serves all.

Everyday's
a field of play!
Serve your time, serve your art.

Thirteen moons.
Twelve months.
Something's been lost.

Find thirteen perfect moons.
Find your art.

E.P.A.

For Liv, Grace, Forrest and Wilden

Our job
as adults

Restore the Earth!

For our children!
E.P.A.
Earth Playground Associates.

Playground Earth!
Earth as playground
not warzone.

Our job:
restory the Earth!

E.P.A. Earth Playground Associates.
Restory the Earth.

WISDOM TEACHERS

The old jazz and blues musicians
    of earlier decades
    have reincarnated
    in the Northern Rockies
    as farting Bison,
    hanging tight together
    in Yellowstone as Bison.
    They have retired
    from the dirty bars
    full of the stenched lives of listeners
    to sulphurously fumed
    picnic grounds
    to the back beats
    of mudpots
    to dark alleys
    and canyoned crevices
    filled with grizzly bears--
    who in the solitary confinement of this life
    enjoy the occasional snorting ruckus of the Bison.

The Bison
    who are digging deep into
    the soil moist with sounds
    of insects digging deep into,
    the bedrock covering
    Yellowstone where the world's
    thinnest crust covers
    the liquid soul of the Earth.

All the old musicians
    living now as Bison
    drop tons of their soft olive bowel
    movements all over the land,
    like poems,
    fertilizing the plains and
    mountains
    clouding streams and skies
    with grunts of glad communion
    with their brethren and   ! cistern !

Herd of Wisdom Teachers?
    Listen for their music.
    It's better than ever.

CHLOROPHYLL

The Earth awakens
to a provider
who is nothing less than
the all-encompassing Source

passing beyond sight
into light
into sound.

The Sun:
orange chlorophyll
spilling earthward.

Plants:
emerald sunlight
break energy into matter.

Converter of Life force.
This is the only enforceable law
around which our world revolves.

Chlorophyll
is Good's will.

ROUTE 287

It is a road of storms
   of high-hailing winds
    and creeks of lightening bolts
    pouring forth the sky.
A prismatic chiming road!
  That's magic
    to know the color of a word
    or the sound a color makes.
It is an A-1 journey
    this road bound from
    Laramie to Ft. Collins
    where states change.
A bypass road
    where I've sat
    inside a rainbow.

I go in hungry each time.
    Oh the lichen's orange song!
    Oh the ponderosa medley!
I go in hungry each time.
    I await this meal,
    this salmon feast of vermilion rock.
It makes me think
   we could eat almost anything
and live
    if we could remember how.

This road of changing states
    links citizens who taste this land
    who take it that personally
    to those who don't
But love this road all the same.
    And the road?
    It works its magic anyway
    on all who pass through.
And that's how change
    comes to bypass
    all sorts of states.

WATCHING THE WEATHER

For Laurie Kutchins

Bring on the Weather!
  Make us stop
and take a long time
  getting to places
and really loving the journey.

Stop us dead in our tracks
  with your power
so we'll no longer be deceived
  by our deception:

That we're in control?

Howl our ears open
  and if you can't with beauty...
then heave ho! Bring on the disasters
  which will widen our eyes.

And if you can't unite us
  with beauty
because we've been made
  so small by life,

then insist we remember.

And do it with rain, with water, with wind in every form
with fire, and lightening, with storms

and rainbows
and hurricanes, earthquakes and
bring on the volcanoes!
It's time the Earth reclaim
Its rightful ownership of Itself!

And if we can't learn by beauty,
then wake us up with the weather,
till all the people get the message
and begin to watch you first again.

And wake us up to your beauty
any way you can.

A LOAD OF REDS

Long have I dreamed of a time
when I'll have a load of reds:
because my nature has ignited,
I am home.
My heart is fully open.

At that time
I'll be wearing black
and few will know
the passion I've achieved
and let go
and burned again.

Like Red-Shafted Flicker
who lands at my door
full of death, full of life
full of living, blood in the feathers.

It's all the same
this life and death
and the color is red
wearing black
and there's no distinction
we are all on fire.

I am alive today
because the dead were living

and through their blood
brought forth the being
that is me.

And we are black and white
and red with life.
Life holds the space
between death
and birth.

And so the medicine:
a load of reds,
so many clothes that hue
because of you
and all the love you brought my way.

EROTICA BASIN

To live bedded down
amongst the lichen
and Bison
without fear.

To disrobe beneath
exposed edges of Earth
sensuous rock
licked by Sun.

To sing the secret songs
emitted from this Earth.

I want to love you
the way I secretly
love the Earth.
I want you to love me
like soft moss
on rocky outcrop.

Our blood
erupting home
toward the heart.

Thank you family and friends.

Special gratitude to
Terry Tempest Williams, Trent Alvey and Laurie Kutchins.
Loving midwives to this book.

Design: Trent Alvey, Salt Lake City, Utah. Paper Stock: cover, 100% recycled with 50% post
consumer waste; fly sheet, 100% post consumer waste; inside, 50 % recycled with 10% post
consumer waste. Printer: Paragon Press, Salt Lake City, Utah.

ABOUT THE AUTHOR

Lyn Dalebout has lived in Grand Teton National Park since 1980.
She has performed her poetry with various groups such as
Grand Teton Music Festival, Greater Yellowstone Coalition
and Dancers' Workshop.
This is her first collection of poetry.